E
YEZ

Yezerski, Thomas.

A full hand.

$16.00

000037156
08/12/2003

DATE			

WITHDRAWN

BAKER & TAYLOR

A FULL HAND

THOMAS F. YEZERSKI

FARRAR STRAUS GIROUX / NEW YORK

For Dad

Thanks to Bob and Linda Barth
and
the Canal Society of New Jersey

Copyright © 2002 by Thomas F. Yezerski

Distributed in Canada by Douglas & McIntyre Ltd.
Color separations by Chroma Graphics PTE Ltd.
Printed and bound in the United States of America by Berryville Graphics
Designed by Filomena Tuosto
First edition, 2002
1 3 5 7 9 10 8 6 4 2

Library of Congress Cataloging-in-Publication Data
Yezerski, Thomas.
   A full hand / Thomas F. Yezerski.— 1st ed.
     p.   cm.
   Summary: Nine-year-old Asa helps his father by leading the mules that
pull his canal boat.
   ISBN 0-374-42502-7
   [1. Canals—Fiction.]   I. Title.

PZ7.Y52 Fu 2002
[E]—dc21

                                        00-140219

FOREWORD

Canals were the highways of nineteenth-century America. Mules could pull a heavy load on a boat much faster than horses pulling a wagon over dirt roads. Canal boats hauled everything from oats to iron ore through America's wilderness.

The canal in this story was inspired by the Morris Canal, which was built mainly to carry coal from Pennsylvania to the harbors of New York and New Jersey, where it could be sold for fuel. The canal stretched over a hundred miles across New Jersey, from Phillipsburg to Jersey City. It climbed mountains and crossed rivers, using inventions like locks, inclined planes, and aqueducts.

A Morris Canal boat was about ten feet wide and ninety feet long. It could be separated into two sections when it had to be filled or go over the top of a hill. There was a stove on deck for cooking and a cabin inside the boat for sleeping. Boatmen sometimes had to live far from home for months at a time.

Two mules would pull the boat, using a long rope, or towline, attached to a towing post on the boat. They followed a dirt walkway, or towpath, next to the canal. The captain steered the boat by moving a handle, or tiller, back and forth. A mule driver stayed with the mules to keep them moving.

By 1900 trains had taken over almost all the work of the Morris Canal, and the waterway was soon abandoned. Remains of it still exist here and there, but most of the canal has disappeared.

One fall evening, Asa was skipping stones on the canal, when his mother and father came down from the house.

"Asa, my mule driver quit today," his father said. "Tomorrow I need you to help me out."

Asa's father was captain of his own canal boat. Folks called him the Captain because he was on his boat for weeks at a time, working hard for his family.

Asa knew a few things about the canal, but he had yet to take a trip. He was only nine, after all.

"How can I help?" Asa asked.

"I'll show you tomorrow," his father said.

"Let's get you packed and ready for bed," his mother said. "You'll need plenty of rest to make your first full hand."

The next morning, Asa's mother called from the kitchen, "Asa, time to wake up!"
It was still dark, but Asa could smell coffee brewing and bread baking. When he
remembered it was going to be his first day on the canal, he shivered. He wasn't sure
if he was cold or afraid. He pulled on his clothes and went downstairs.

"Come and feed the mules with me, Asa," the Captain said. "We can eat after they do."

"Yes, sir," Asa said. They walked to the stable, where Asa scooped oats into the feed bags. The Captain lifted the bags over the mules' heads. Then Asa and his father headed back to the house to eat a couple of bowls of oatmeal themselves.

After breakfast, the Captain said, "Let's get a move on. We have to pick up our load at the coal chutes and get it to Jersey City in five days."

Asa's mother walked with them to the boat. She took Asa aside. "You know, Asa," she said quietly, "your father was a mule driver once, too, though you would never guess it. You're going to do just fine." She hugged him tightly. Asa smiled, and hugged her back.

The Captain tied one end of the towline to the mules' harnesses. He tied the other end to a towing post on the deck.

"Asa," he said, "your job is to lead the mules, just like you do when you put them in the stable. Keep them moving. Don't let them stray off the towpath, or they will drag the boat into the bank."

All of a sudden, the mules looked awfully big to Asa.

The Captain took his place by the tiller at the back of the boat. "Ready?" he called.

"Ready!" Asa answered, doing his best to sound ready.

"Walk on!" the Captain commanded. The mules leaned forward, and the towline sprang straight. The boat creaked to life.

The Captain pushed the tiller to the right to steer the boat into the middle of the canal. Asa walked with the mules, his hand holding the harness, but the animals already knew what to do. Their hooves clapped softly on the ground, and the water rippled past the boat.

"See you in a couple of weeks!" called Asa's mother.

At the coal chutes, trains whistled and clanged, men yelled, and coal roared into wooden hulls. Asa was thrilled.

"Stay here and hold on to the mules while I fill the boat," the Captain shouted.

Asa halted the mules, and the Captain untied the towline from the boat. Asa watched him guide the boat to the chutes with a pike pole. Dockworkers helped his father unhinge the two sections of the boat, so they could fill both halves at the same time.

When the sections were lined up, coal poured out of railroad cars, down the chutes, and into the sections. The dockworkers moved the chutes back and forth to fill the sections evenly. When they were full, the Captain hinged them together again and pushed the boat back to Asa and the mules. Asa threw the towline to him as hard as he could. "Good throw!" said the Captain. He tied it to the towing post on the boat, and they were on their way.

After a couple of hours, Asa settled in to the mules' easy pace. They passed a cornfield, and one mule started to wander off the path. Asa yelled, "Come on! You had breakfast!" She swished her tail and knocked Asa's hat off.

"You have to show them who's boss, Asa," the Captain said, laughing.

"Let's go! We have to keep moving!" Asa scolded, grabbing the lead mule by the bit.

The Captain lifted a big conch shell to his mouth and blew on it like a horn.

Asa was startled by its loud wail. "What's that for?" he asked.

"There's a lock ahead," said the Captain. "I have to signal the lock tender that we're coming. The next part of the canal is higher than the part we're on now. The lock will lift the boat to the higher level."

The canal flowed into the lock through a set of miter gates, like doors. The Captain untied the towline and let the boat coast through the gates. The lock tender tied a rope from the boat to a snubbing post, and the boat squeaked to a stop. Children ran up to watch the boat go through the lock.

"Stand!" Asa ordered the mules, and they stopped.

"Morning, Mrs. Dailey," the Captain said, tipping his hat. "How's the finest baker and lock tender in Warren County?"

Mrs. Dailey laughed. "I'm fine. I see you have a new mule driver today. You must be Asa."

"Yes, ma'am," Asa said.

"Well, I sure am pleased to meet you," said Mrs. Dailey as she turned a crank above the miter gates to close them. "I've heard a lot about you."

Then Mrs. Dailey walked to the other end of the lock. She opened paddle gates to fill the lock with water. Asa watched the boat rise up until it was as high as the upper level of the canal.

"Boy!" Asa exclaimed. "That's some trick, ma'am!"

Mrs. Dailey smiled. "Captain, how about you take along a pumpkin pie for your new driver?" she asked.

"Well, how can we turn down an offer like that?" the Captain said. "Thank you!"

Mrs. Dailey's daughter brought them a pie. While the Captain tied the towline to the towing post, Mrs. Dailey pushed the huge drop gate down, so the boat could float over it. Asa yelled, "Walk on!" and the mules pulled the boat out of the lock and away.

The boat wound through fields and forests. They even crossed a stream on an aqueduct, which was a bridge with the canal built right into it.

Asa kept the mules moving with a word or just a pat of his hand.

The Captain called, "I see they're not giving you much trouble anymore."

"Oh, they're all right," Asa answered. He smiled to himself.

Up ahead, the canal seemed to end at the foot of a high hill.

"This is an inclined plane," said the Captain, "and we're going up."

Asa couldn't imagine how. He saw a cradle car in the water, at the bottom of the hill. The Captain floated the boat onto it and then leaped off. Inside a tower, the plane tender opened a door to let water from the canal through a flume. The rushing water turned a wheel, and the wheel pulled a cable connected to the cradle car.

Asa and the Captain climbed the plane together with the mules. They ate pieces of pumpkin pie as the countryside fell around them. "I bet all the other kids are just playing tag and checkers today," Asa said. The Captain put a hand on Asa's shoulder.

At the top of the hill the cradle car splashed into the canal again. The Captain jumped aboard and tied the towline. Asa prodded the mules, and they pulled the boat off the car.

Late in the afternoon a breeze picked up. The mules' ears twitched. Asa turned around and saw the angriest black clouds he had ever seen. A deep roll of thunder shook the air. The Captain turned and saw the clouds, too.

"Hold tight!" he shouted.

Suddenly, a shimmering wall of rain fell, and almost immediately Asa was soaked through. Lightning struck a tree, and the mules reared up in fright. They screamed and kicked and tried to get away.

"No!" cried Asa. "Stay on the path! Stay on the path!" He grabbed the reins, but the mules just dragged him along. They tugged the boat closer and closer to the bank.

"Hang on!" the Captain yelled. He thrust the pike pole into the canal floor and vaulted to the towpath, just in time to yank Asa out of the way of the thrashing mules. He hurried to unhitch the towline from the harnesses, but it was too late.

Crash! The boat hit the rocks along the side of the canal. *Snap!* The towline broke. The mules kicked wildly. One kick caught the Captain's leg, sending him stumbling and sliding into the flooding canal.

Frightened, Asa searched the canal for his father. All he could see through the curtains of rain was the crippled boat drifting backward on the current. Lightning flashed again, and he saw that the Captain was caught in the rushing water! Asa felt helpless, but then he remembered the pike pole. Scrambling through the mud, he found it and raced downstream, faster than the current.

When he passed his father, Asa threw himself to the ground and stretched the pole over the water. The Captain grabbed it as he floated past. Asa put all his weight on the pole, and the Captain pulled himself out of the canal.

Asa and the Captain sat on the bank. The storm cloud drifted away, leaving a muddy mess behind. The boat was smashed and wedged into the bank. The mules had fled.

"That storm nearly got the best of us," the Captain said.

"That was something else when you vaulted off the boat," Asa said.

"You were pretty handy with that pole yourself," the Captain replied.

"Shouldn't we go look for the mules or pull the boat out?" asked Asa.

"We can do all that tomorrow. I'm sure the mules found a farm nearby, and we're going to need a lot of help fixing the boat. In the meantime, there's a village up ahead where we can get some supper and sleep."

Asa helped his father up. The Captain leaned on his son as they limped down the towpath.

"I think I'd like to be a captain someday, too, Dad."

"I think you'll be able to do anything you set your mind to, Asa," answered the Captain.

The tired boatmen came to the inn. They had two bowls of beef stew apiece. Then they went to bed. Before the sun rose on the canal again, Asa and the Captain had already started a new day.